CORNELIUS GUS

Written by **ROCCO SIMARI**   Illustrated by **AMY DESCHENE**

Copyright ©2009 by Rocco Simari.

Library of Congress Control Number: 2009905973

ISBN-13: 978-0-9840787-2-1

ISBN-10: 0-9840787-2-x

Editor: M. Coleen Driscoll Simari

Copy Editor: Lisa Morris

Book and cover designed by: Steven Deschene

www.RoccoSimari.com

www.SpeedwellPublishing.com

Printed in America

*Katie
Embrace reading!
Rocco Simari
"09"*

Cornelius and Gus were a couple of friends.
They were friends for a very long time.

One day they decided to go on a journey,
and got on a train for the ride.

Along with their luggage they took,
some bread, some cheese, and a bottle of wine.

For breakfast or lunch or just to munch,
and help them across the divide.

It was an old train with old wooden seats,
that made them rock all around.

They couldn't wait for the end of this trip,
so they would be back on the ground.

Down by the seacoast and over the bridge,
along the mountainside.

They traveled through tunnels and slept all night,
to get to the end of this ride.

Just before dawn, as the light came in,
they woke up to the sound of a horn.

They stopped at the dockside and got on a ship,
that took them away from home.

They got on board and stood at the stern,
as they waved at their home goodbye.

There were tears in their eyes, as the ship sailed away,
and hoped to be back by her side.

It was a long trip that lasted for days.
The ocean was fierce, the waves were ferocious.

The weather was rough, it was cold, it was raining.
They were told about this from the very beginning.

They stopped at some places and visited natives,
of countries and islands between.

They found wonderful treasures and beautiful faces,
they never knew or had seen.

As the end of the journey was nearing,
they stood at the bow of the ship.

They glanced at the coast to see the new land,
and the people they've been waiting to meet.

The closer they got the better they felt,
to see people and buildings nearby.

As twilight was coming there were beautiful lights,
so many that lit up the sky.

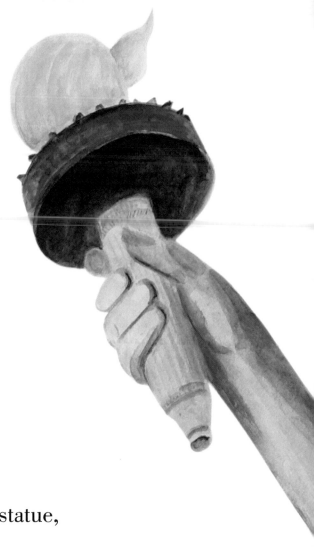

They suddenly glanced at the beautiful statue,
that was proudly standing nearby.

A symbol of freedom to welcome newcomers,
with glory, greatness, and pride.

The end of the journey was coming so fast,
for Gus and Cornelius a new life to start.

The past are just memories they'll never forget,
this is their new home, their new home at last.

I dedicate this book to my father, Alfredo Simari,
who was the first in the family to make this voyage to America.

Author's Biography

Rocco earned his degree in secondary education and always dreamed of writing stories for children. In the past Rocco has worked as a designer, builder, and substitute teacher while raising a family of four with his wife Coleen. Coleen is a Language Arts teacher who's had a lot of great input in Rocco's stories. Cornelius and Gus stemmed from his own experience when he came to America with his family at the age of nine. Rocco, Coleen and their four children presently reside at their family home in Southern New Hampshire.

Illustrator's Biography

Amy's love for her two children and passion for art has made the road to illustrating children's books very enjoyable. Amy spent her childhood growing up in beautiful Vermont, and she has always been inspired by the seasonal colors of New England. Today, Amy enjoys teaching young artists at a middle school in New Hampshire.

Other books by Rocco Simari

Little Nick
The Cynical Cyclone (coming soon)

www.RoccoSimari.com
www.SpeedwellPublishing.com

Printed in the United States
153237LV00002B

9780984078721